FIVE MINUTE
Bedtime Tales

FIVE MINUTE
Bedtime Tales

Written by
Derek Hall, Alison Morris
and Louisa Somerville

DP
DEMPSEY
PARR

Illustrated by
Jeremy Bays, Lynn Breeze, Maureen Galvani, Mary Hall,
Virginia Margerison, Paula Martyr, Julia Oliver, Martin Orme,
Gillian Toft, Kerry Vaughan, Jenny Williams, Kirsty Wilson

Cover illustrated by Julia Oliver

Designed by Louise Millar

First published in Great Britain in 1998 by
DEMPSEY PARR, 13 Whiteladies Road
Clifton, Bristol BS8 1PB

Copyright © 1998 PARRAGON

Created and produced for DEMPSEY PARR by
Linda Watters Book Packaging
8 Trent Close, Shenley
Herts WD7 9HX, UK

ISBN 1-84084-335-7

Printed in Singapore

Contents

The Invisible Imp

One day, Sarah Jones was pegging out her washing. It was a lovely day and she was looking forward to visiting her friend Rose. "I'll just get this washing on the line while the sun's shining," she said to herself, "and then I'll be on my way."

After a while, she stopped and looked down into the basket. "That's very peculiar!" she thought. "I know I've already pegged out that green shirt and there it is back in the basket." She carried on pegging out the clothes. Now she shook her head in disbelief. For although she had been working away for quite a while, the basket of washing was still full and there was almost nothing on the line! She began to get quite cross, for she was going to be late getting to Rose's house.

Try as she might, she just could not get that washing pegged. In the end, she had to leave the basket of wet washing and run to Rose's house.

"I'm so sorry I'm late, Rose," she gasped, all out of breath from running. Sarah told Rose all about what had happened.

"Well," said Rose, "that's a strange coincidence. I was baking some cakes for us to have for tea. Every time I put them in the oven and turned away, they were out of the oven and on the table again! In the end I had to stand guard over them – which reminds me, they were just beginning to cook nicely when you knocked on the door."

The two women went into Rose's kitchen and there were the cakes, sitting on the table again, half-cooked. "Now they're ruined!" cried Rose. "Whatever shall we do?"

At that moment, there was a noise in the street. Rose and Sarah looked out of the window to see Elmer, the mailman, surrounded by a crowd of people all shouting and waving envelopes in the air. The two women ran out into the street. "What's going on?" they cried.

"Elmer's given us all the wrong mail," said Rose's neighbor, Dora. "He's normally so reliable, but this morning he seems to have gone completely crazy. Now we've got to sort out all the mail for him."

"I don't know what's happened," wailed Elmer in anguish. "I'm sure I posted all the letters through the right doors."

"Well," said Sarah, "Rose and I have also found strange things happening to us this morning." She told the crowd their stories. Everyone forgave Elmer when they realised it wasn't his fault, but they were still truly mystified as to what – or who – could have caused all these problems.

But that wasn't the end of it. Oh no, indeed! The butcher's wife served her family mutton stew, but when she lifted the lid the family heard a bleating sound and a little lamb leaped out of the pot. The milkman delivered the milk as usual, but when people took their milk indoors, they found the bottles were full of lemonade. Old Mr Smith tried to pull his chair up to the table and found it was stuck hard to the floor. And when Mrs Smith painted her bedroom blue, she came back and found it had changed to pink with purple spots.

Can you guess what had happened? Do you know who'd been up to all these tricks? It was an imp, of course! The wicked little fellow had become bored playing pranks on the fairies and goblins in fairyland. By now, they knew all his tricks and he was finding it harder and harder to catch them out. Then he had an idea. Why not play tricks in the human world where he would be invisible? So that's exactly what he did.

At first, he really only meant
to play one or two tricks, but he
had such fun that he couldn't
resist carrying on.

Well, the invisible imp continued
on with his tricks. But of course, as you know,
pride comes before a fall, and one day he just went too far. Sarah
Jones had been invited to a party. It was to be a fancy dress party
and on the invitation it said: "*Please wear red*". Now Sarah
fretted because she had no red clothes at all. Then she
had an idea. She got out an old blue frock from the
back of the closet. "I'll dye it red," she thought.

She mixed a big tub of red dye and was just about to put the
dress into it, when along came the invisible imp. "Here's some
fun!" he thought. "I'll turn the dye blue. Then she won't know
why her dress hasn't changed color. Won't that be funny!" And
he started giggling to himself at the thought of it. He danced up
and down on the edge of the tub, thinking up
a really evil spell to turn the dye blue.

But he laughed so much to himself
that he slipped and fell right into
the bright red mixture. Fast as
lightning out he scrambled
and cast his spell.

10

Sure enough Sarah fished out the dress from the tub, and to her dismay saw that it was exactly the same color as when she had put it into the dye. She was about to peer into the tub when something caught her eye. For there, sitting on the table, chuckling to himself and holding his sides with laughter, was a bright red imp. And there was a trail of tiny red footprints from the tub of dye to the table. The silly imp had no idea that he was no longer invisible and that Sarah could see him as plain as the nose on her face! In a flash Sarah realized what had happened. She chased the imp out of the house and down the street and, I'm glad to say, he wasn't able to play his mischievous tricks ever again.

11

Peter Meets a Dragon

Once upon a time there was a young boy named Peter. He lived in an ordinary house with an ordinary Mum and Dad, an ordinary sister and an ordinary pet cat, called Jasper. In fact, everything in Peter's life was so ordinary that he sometimes wished that something extraordinary would happen. "Why doesn't a giant come and squash the house flat with his foot?" he wondered, and "If only a pirate would take my sister hostage!" But each day, Peter would wake up in the morning and everything was just the same as it had been the day before.

One morning Peter woke up to find a very strange smell in the house. Looking out of his bedroom window, he saw that the front lawn was scorched and blackened. There was smoke drifting off the grass and, further away, he could see some bushes ablaze.

Peter rushed downstairs and out of the front door. He ran out of the garden and down the lane following the trail of smoke and burning grass. He grew more and more puzzled, however, as there was no sign of anything that could have caused such a blaze.

Peter was about to run home and tell his Mom and Dad, when he heard a panting noise coming from the undergrowth. Parting the bushes gently with his hands he found a young creature. It had green, scaly skin, a pair of wings and a long snout full of sharp teeth. Every now and again a little tongue of flame came from its nostrils, setting the grass around it on fire. "A baby dragon!" Peter said to himself, in great surprise. Big tears were rolling out of the dragon's yellow eyes and down its scaly cheeks as it flapped its wings desperately and tried to take off.

When the dragon saw Peter it stopped flapping its wings. "Oh, woe is me!" it sobbed. "Where am I?"

"Where do you want to be?" asked Peter, kneeling down on the scorched ground.

"I want to be in Dragonland with my friends," replied the dragon. "We were all flying together, but I just couldn't keep up with them. I got tired and needed a rest. I called to the others but they didn't hear me. Then I just had to stop and get my breath back. Now I don't know where I am, or if I'll ever see my friends again!" And with that the baby dragon started to cry once more.

"I'm sure I can help. I'll get you home," said Peter, though he had no idea how.

"You?" hissed a voice nearby. "How could you possibly help? You're just a boy!" Peter looked round, and to his astonishment found Jasper sitting behind him. "I suppose you're going to wave a magic wand, are you?" continued Jasper. "You need to call in an expert." Then he turned his back on Peter and the baby dragon and started washing his paws.

Peter was astounded. He'd never heard Jasper talking before. He had thought he was just an ordinary pet cat. "W… w… what do you mean?" he stammered.

"Well," said Jasper, glancing over his shoulder at Peter, "I reckon that horse over there could help. Follow me."

So Peter and the baby dragon – whose name was Flame – followed Jasper over to where the horse stood at the edge of a field. Jasper leaped up on to the gate and called to the horse. Then he whispered in the horse's ear. The horse thought for a moment, then whispered back in Jasper's ear. "He says he's got a friend on the other side of the wood who'll help," said Jasper.

"But how?" said Peter, looking perplexed.

"Be patient! Follow me!" said Jasper as he stalked off through the grass. "And tell your friend to stop setting fire to everything!" he added. Peter saw, to his horror, that Flame was indeed blazing a trail through the field.

"I can't help it," cried Flame, about to burst into tears again. "Every time I get out of breath I start to pant, and then I start breathing fire."

"Let me carry you," said Peter. He picked Flame up in his arms and ran after Jasper. The baby dragon felt very strange. His body was all cold and clammy, but his mouth was still breathing hot smoke, which made Peter's eyes water.

He ran through the wood, just keeping Jasper's upright tail in sight. On the other side of the wood was another field, and in the field was a horse. But this was no ordinary horse. Peter stopped dead in his tracks and stared. The horse was pure milky white, and from its head grew a single, long horn. "A unicorn!" breathed Peter.

Jasper was already talking to the unicorn. He beckoned with his paw to Peter. "He'll take your friend home and you can go, too, Peter, but don't be late for tea, or you know what your mom will say." And with that, Jasper was off.

"Climb aboard," said the unicorn gently.

Peter and the little dragon scrambled up on to the unicorn's back. "What an adventure," thought Peter. Up, up, and away they soared through the clouds.

Flame held tightly on to Peter's hand with his clammy paw. At last Peter could see a mountain ahead through the clouds. Now they were descending through the clouds again, and soon the unicorn landed right at the top of the mountain. "I'm home!" squeaked Flame joyously as they landed. Sure enough, several dragons were running over to greet him. They looked quite friendly, but some of them were rather large and one was breathing a great deal of fire.

"Time for me to go," said Peter a little nervously, as Flame jumped off the unicorn's back and flew to the ground. The unicorn took off again and soon they were back in the field once more.

As he slid off the unicorn's back, Peter turned to thank him, but when he looked he saw that it was just an ordinary horse with no trace of a horn at all. Peter walked back home across the field, but there was no sign of burnt grass. He reached his own front lawn, which was also in perfect condition. Peter felt more and more perplexed. "I hope Jasper can explain," he thought, as the cat ran past him and into the house. "Jasper, I took the baby dragon home. What's happened to the burnt grass?" he blurted out. But Jasper said not a word. He ignored Peter and curled up in his basket.

When Peter wasn't looking, however, Jasper gave him a glance that seemed to say, "Well, was that a big enough adventure for you?"

Lucy and the Green Door

Lucy Jenkins lived in an ordinary house, in an ordinary street, in an ordinary town. At the back of Lucy's house was an ordinary backyard with ordinary flowers and an ordinary path. But down the path at the bottom of the backyard was a tree that was not ordinary at all! It was a huge old oak tree, and at the bottom of the tree was a very small green door, only just big enough for Lucy to squeeze through. This was Lucy's secret, because only she knew about the door. But what lay behind the door was Lucy's best secret of all!

Each afternoon Lucy would go down the path and knock lightly on the door. On the third knock the door would swing open wide, and the chief elf would be there to welcome her inside.

"Come inside, little Lucy," the elf would always say, "and have some tea."

Inside, Lucy would meet some very special friends indeed! First there were Penelope and Geraldine, two of the gentlest and sweetest fairies it was possible to imagine. Then there were Basil and Granville, who were rather mischievous imps (but who made Lucy laugh with their tricks and jokes), and there were the storytellers, who would sit for hours with Lucy and tell her the greatest tales from all the corners of the world. And of course there was the chief elf, who would make the most delicious milkshakes and scones with heaps of cream for Lucy to eat.

The world behind the green door was a wonderful place, and Lucy would always go home afterwards feeling very cheerful and jolly. On one particular visit to the world behind the green door Lucy had just finished a scrumptious tea of cocoa and toasted marshmallows with the chief elf, when she went off to play games with Basil and Granville. They were playing blind man's buff, and Lucy roared with laughter as Basil sneaked up on the blindfolded Granville and tickled him in the ribs, making him squeal and beg for the teasing to stop.

19

Now just recently, Lucy had been feeling very blue because very soon she would be going to school and would only be able to visit her friends at weekends. But they assured her that they would never forget her, and that as long as she was always a true friend to them she could visit as often or as little as she liked. This cheered Lucy up considerably, and then they took her to visit the storytellers so that her happiness was complete. Of all the delights behind the green door, the storytellers were Lucy's favorite. They told her stories of how the whales had learned to sing, and of where the stars went when the sun had risen in the sky and they had slipped from view.

Because of the assurances of the fairies, Lucy was not too worried when the day finally came for her to join all the other boys and girls of her age at school. Every day, Lucy would go to school and then afterwards would visit her friends behind the green door. As winter came round and the days grew dark she only visited at weekends, and looked forward to the vacations when she could visit them every day once more.

Meanwhile, at school, Lucy had made friends with a girl called Jessica, and although she told Jessica all about her family and her home, she didn't at first tell her about her extraordinary tree with the little green door and the magic world that lay beyond. Lucy did tell Jessica all the stories that she was told by the storytellers, however, and Jessica grew more and more curious about where she had heard all the wonderful tales. Every day, Jessica would ask more and more questions, and Lucy found it more and more difficult to avoid telling her about her secret. Eventually, Lucy gave in and told Jessica all about her adventures behind the green door.

Jessica scoffed and laughed when Lucy told her about the chief elf, and Basil, Granville, Penelope and Geraldine. She howled with laughter at the thought of the wonderful teas and the stories that followed. Jessica thought that Lucy was making the whole thing up! When Lucy protested, and said it was true, Jessica told her that it simply wasn't possible – that there were no such things as elves and fairies and imps and strange and wonderful worlds behind doors in trees. Lucy was distraught, and decided to take Jessica to the green door.

On the way home Lucy started to worry. What if she really had imagined it all? But if her wonderful friends didn't exist, how could she possibly know them? Jessica walked beside Lucy, still teasing her and laughing about Lucy's 'invisible' friends!

When Lucy and Jessica reached the bottom of the backyard, Lucy was about to tap lightly on the green door at the bottom of the oak tree when she suddenly noticed the door had disappeared. She rubbed her eyes and looked again, but it simply wasn't there!

Jessica smirked and laughed at Lucy, calling her silly and babyish to believe in magic and fairy tales, and then ran off back down the road to school. Lucy could not face going back to school that afternoon, and when her mother saw her enter the house she thought she must be ill – she looked so upset! Lucy went to bed early and cried herself to sleep.

And when Lucy slept she started to dream. The chief elf, Basil and Granville, Penelope and Geraldine and the storytellers were all there in the dream. Then Penelope and Geraldine stepped forward and hugged Lucy, and the hug was so real that

Lucy began to hope it wasn't a dream! Then
they all hugged her and asked why she
hadn't been to see them for so long, and
why they had not been able to reach
out to her except now in the deepest
of sleeps. Lucy explained what had happened
on her last visit, and told them all about Jessica, and
then Geraldine spoke. "Little Lucy," she said, "you are special.
You believe in magic and you believe in the little people. And
because you believe, you are able to see us and live among us.
But those who don't believe will always be shut out from our
world. You must keep your belief, little Lucy."

With a huge surge of happiness Lucy woke up, dressed quickly
and ran out of her ordinary house, down the ordinary path in the
ordinary backyard up to the extraordinary tree, and was delighted
to see the green door once more! She knocked very lightly and,
after the third tap, the door opened to reveal the chief elf. "Come
inside, little Lucy," the elf said happily, "and have some tea."

Esmerelda the Ragdoll

At the back of the toy closet on a dark and dusty shelf lay
Esmerelda the ragdoll. She lay on her back and stared at the shelf
above, as she had done for a very long time. It seemed to
Esmerelda that it was many years since she had been lifted up by
Clara, her owner, and even longer since she had been out in the
playroom with the other toys. Now her lovely yellow hair was all
tangled and her beautiful blue dress was creased, torn and faded.
Each time Clara opened the toy closet door, Esmerelda hoped
very much that she would be chosen, but Clara always played
with the newer toys at the front of the closet. Every time Clara
put her toys back in the closet, Esmerelda felt herself being
pushed further towards the back. It was very uncomfortable and
indeed, Esmerelda might have suffocated if it wasn't for a hole at
the back of the closet, which enabled her to breathe.

These days Esmerelda felt very lonely. Until recently a one-eyed teddy bear had been beside her on the shelf. Then one day he had fallen through the hole at the back of the closet and was never seen again. Esmerelda missed him dreadfully, for he had been a lovely old teddy with a gentle nature. Now she, too, could feel herself being pushed towards the hole. She felt a mixture of excitement and fright at the prospect of falling through it. Sometimes she imagined that she would land on a soft feather bed belonging to a little girl who would really love her. At other times she thought that the hole led to a terrifying land full of monsters.

One day Esmerelda heard Clara's mother say, "Now Clara, today you must tidy up the toy closet and clear out all those old toys you no longer play with."

Esmerelda could see Clara's small hands reaching into the closet. She couldn't bear the thought of being picked up by the little girl and then discarded. "There's only one thing to do," she said to herself. She wriggled towards the hole, closed her eyes and jumped. Esmerelda felt herself falling, and then she landed with a bump on something soft.

"Watch out, my dear!" said a familiar voice from underneath her. Esmerelda opened her eyes and saw that she had landed on One-eyed Ted.

The two toys were so overjoyed to see each other again that they hugged one another. "What shall we do now?" cried Esmerelda.

"I have an idea," said Ted. "There's a rusty old toy automobile over there. I wanted to escape in it, but I can't drive with only one eye. What do you think? Shall we give it a go?"

"Yes, yes!" exclaimed Esmerelda, climbing into the driver's seat.

By now One-eyed Ted had found the key and was winding up the automobile. "Away we go!" he called as they sped off.

"Where are we going?" shouted Esmerelda.

"To the seaside," replied Ted.

"Which way is it?" asked Esmerelda, holding on to her yellow hair streaming behind her in the wind.

"I don't know. We'll have to ask the way," said Ted.

Rounding a bend, they came across a black cat crossing the road. "Excuse me," called Ted, "could you tell us the way to the seaside?"

Now, as you know, cats hate water. "Whatever do they want to go near water for? Why should I help them?" thought the cat. "It's the other side of that mountain," he growled as he ran off.

On sped the rusty automobile, and up the mountainside. When they reached the top of the mountain they met a sheep. Now, as you know, sheep never listen properly. "Excuse me," said Esmerelda, "where can we find the beach?"

Well, the silly sheep thought Esmerelda was asking where they could find a peach! "Down there," she bleated, nodding towards an orchard in the valley below.

Esmerelda and Ted leaped back into the automobile and sped off down the mountainside, but when they reached the orchard there was no sign of water, of course – just a lot of peach trees.

Once again they scratched their heads in puzzlement.
Just then a mole popped his head out of the earth.
"Excuse me," said Ted, "would you happen to
know how we can find the seaside?"

Now the mole was very wise, but
unfortunately he was also, as you
know, very short sighted. He peered at Esmerelda's blue dress.
"That patch of blue must surely be a river, and rivers run into
the sea," he thought.

"Just follow that river," he said, "and you'll end up at the seaside.
Good day!" And with that he disappeared under ground again.

Esmerelda and Ted looked even more puzzled, for there was
no sign of a river in the orchard. "Oh well," sighed Esmerelda,
"perhaps we'll never find the seaside."

"Don't give up," said Ted. "We'll surely find it in the end." They
climbed back in the rusty car and set off again. After a short while
the car started to splutter and then it came to a complete halt at
the side of the road. "What shall we do now?" cried Esmerelda.

"We'll just have to wait here and see what happens," said Ted.
It seemed like a very long time that they sat beside the road. At
long last they heard footsteps, and then Esmerelda felt herself
being picked up.

"Look – it's a dear old tatty ragdoll," said a voice. Esmerelda
looked up and saw that she was being carried by a little girl.

Ted and the automobile were picked up by the girl's father. "We'll take them home and look after them," the man said.

Now they were in a real automobile and soon the toys found themselves in a house. The little girl carried Esmerelda, One-eyed Ted and the rusty automobile to her bedroom and put them down on a window sill. "I'll be back soon," she whispered.

Esmerelda looked out of the window and nearly danced for joy. "Look, look Ted," she shouted. For out of the window she could see the road, and beyond the road was a beach and then the sea. "We reached the seaside after all," she cried.

Esmerelda, Ted and the rusty automobile lived happily in the house beside the sea. Esmerelda's hair was brushed and plaited and she was given a beautiful new dress. Ted had a new eye sewn on and could see properly again. The rusty automobile was painted and oiled. Most days the little girl took her new toys down to the beach to play with, and the days in the dark toy closet were soon forgotten. The little girl used to tell her friends the story of how she had found her three best toys lying beside the road one day. And as for the toys, well, they sometimes talked about that strange day when they had such an adventure – and they'd burst out laughing.

The Giant Who Shrank

Once upon a time in a far-off land, there lived a huge giant.
He made his home in a big cave high up in the mountains.
His bed, table and chairs were made from great tree trunks.
And when he wanted a drink, he simply filled an old bath tub
with water and drank it down in one enormous gulp.
When he snored – which he did almost every night –
it sounded like a huge thunderstorm,
and the noise echoed all
around the mountains.

At the bottom of the mountains there was a village, but all
the folk in the village were very different from the giant, for they
were not big at all. They were just like you and me. They were
afraid of the giant, of course, and whenever he came striding
down the mountains to hunt, they all ran away into the woods
or locked themselves inside their houses. Sometimes, the clumsy
giant would tramp around the village squashing houses with his
great feet as he went, and that only made the village folk even
more frightened of him!

Although the giant was so big and strong, he was not a bad giant, but he was very, very lonely because everyone ran away whenever he appeared. Sometimes, while he was sitting alone in his cave, he could hear the villagers having feasts and parties and he longed to join them and be just like them.

One day, when the giant was tramping around the village as usual, something glinting in the sun caught his eye. At the top of a big tree (which of course was not very big as far as the giant was concerned) lay a gold box.

32

The giant bent down and picked up the box. To his surprise he heard a small voice inside say, "Help! Help! Let me out!"

The giant opened the box and out jumped an elf. "Thank you, thank you, large sir," he said. "I am a magic elf, but one of my spells went wrong and I got locked inside this box. No-one in the village could hear me calling for help high up in this tree."

To show his thanks, the elf said he would grant the giant one wish.

"I wish I could be the same as all the other villagers," boomed the giant.

"What a difficult wish," said the elf. "You are so big! But I will do my best." The elf closed his eyes and chanted a magic spell. But nothing seemed to happen – the giant was still as big as ever.

The giant was very sad to
discover that he had not shrunk,
but he wished the elf well, thanked
him for trying and went on his way.
As the giant was walking back to his
cave in the mountains, he noticed
something strange. All the puddles
of water that he had passed on the
way down to the village had got
bigger. They were as big as lakes
now! The giant looked up to see if
it had been raining, but the sky
was clear and blue.

Then another strange thing
happened. The big stone steps
he had cut in the mountain side
leading up to his cave had also
got bigger! He could hardly
clamber up them.

Eventually, puffing and panting,
the giant reached the door to his
cave. But he could not reach the
door knob. It now towered
above him, far from his reach.

"What is happening?" thought the giant. "The elf's spell must have gone wrong. Not only am I still a giant, but everything around me has now got even bigger."

Suddenly the truth came to him. Of course! Everything had not become bigger – he had become smaller! The spell had worked after all. Now he was just the same as the other folk in the village.

He made his way to the village, wondering if everyone would still run away as before. But he need not have worried. All the village folk welcomed him into the village, and he lived there happily among them for the rest of his days.

Rusty's Big Day

Long ago there lived a poor farmer called Fred, who had a horse called Rusty. Once Rusty had been a good, strong horse. He had willingly pulled the plow and taken his master into town to sell his vegetables. Now he was too old to work on the farm, but the farmer couldn't bear to think of getting rid of him because he was so sweet-natured. "It would be like turning away one of my own family," Fred used to say. Rusty spent his days grazing in the corner of the field. He was quite content, but he felt sad that he was no longer able to help the poor farmer earn his living.

One day, Fred decided to go to town to sell a few vegetables. He harnessed Beauty, the young mare, to the wagon and off they went. Beauty shook her fine mane and tossed a glance at Rusty as if to say, "Look who's queen of the farmyard!"

While Fred was in the town, his eye was caught by a notice pinned to a tree. It said:

> Horse Parade at 2 pm today
> The winner will pull the king's carriage
> to the Grand Banquet tonight

"There's not a moment to lose, my girl!" said Fred. "We must get you ready for the parade." So saying, he turned the wagon around. "Giddy-up, Beauty!" he called, and she trotted all the way back to the farm.

Fred set to work to make Beauty look more lovely than she had ever done before. He scrubbed her hoofs and brushed her coat until it shone. Then he plaited her mane and tied it with a bright red ribbon. Rusty watched from the field. "How fine she looks," he thought, wistfully. "She's sure to win." He felt a bit sad that he was too old to take part in the parade, so he found a patch of the sweetest grass to graze on, to console himself.

All at once, he heard Fred approach. "Come on, old boy," he said, "you can come, too. It'll be fun for you to watch the parade, won't it?" Rusty was thrilled. It seemed such a long time since the master had last taken him into town. Fred brushed Rusty's coat, too.

"You want to look your best, don't you now, old boy?" he said. Soon the three of them set off back into town, with Fred riding on Beauty's back and Rusty walking by their side. When they reached the parade ground, there were already a lot of horses gathered there with their owners. There were horses of every shape and size – small, skinny ones, big, muscular ones and there were even big, skinny ones, too!

Soon it was time for the parade to begin. The king entered the parade ground, followed by the members of the royal court. They took their places at one end of the ground. Then the king announced three contests. First there would be a race. The horses would gallop from one end of the parade ground to the other. Then there would be a contest of strength. Each horse would have to try and pull a heavy carriage. Lastly, there would be a trotting competition. Each horse would have to carry a rider around the parade ground.

The competition began. All the horses lined up at the starting line. "Come on, Rusty. Have a go!" whispered Fred. He led Rusty and Beauty to where the other horses were lined up.

All the other horses turned and stared. "What's an old horse like you doing taking part in a contest like this?" one of them asked disdainfully.

"You won't make it past the starting line!" taunted another.

Rusty said nothing and took his place at the start. Then they were off down the field. Rusty felt his heart pounding and his feet fly like never before, but try as he might he just couldn't keep up with the others and came in last.

"What did you expect?" snorted the other horses turning their backs on poor old Rusty.

However, Rusty was not downcast. "Speed isn't everything," he said to himself.

Now it was time for the test of strength. One by one the horses took it in turns to pull the carriage. When it was Rusty's turn, he tried his best. He felt every muscle in his aching body strain, as he slowly pulled the carriage along.

"Not a hope!" declared the other horses.

"Strength isn't everything," said Rusty to himself.

Next it was time for the trotting competition. "I shall ride each horse in turn," declared the king. He climbed up on to the first horse, but it bolted away so fast that the king was left hanging by the stirrups. The next horse lifted his legs so high that he threw the king right up in the air and he might have hurt himself badly, if he hadn't been caught by one of his courtiers. The next horse was so nervous about carrying the king that his teeth chattered, and the king had to put his fingers in his ears. Then it was Beauty's turn and she carried the king magnificently, until she stumbled at the end. At last it was Rusty's turn. The other horses sniggered, "Let's see that old horse make a fool of himself!"

Rusty carried the king quite slowly and steadily, making sure he picked his feet up carefully, so that his royal highness would not be jolted. "Thank you for a most pleasant ride," said the king dismounting. There was a hush as the horses and their owners awaited the result of the contest. "I have decided," announced the king, "that Rusty is the winner. Not only did he give me a most comfortable ride, but he accepted his other defeats with dignity. Speed and strength are not everything, you know."

Rusty and Fred were overjoyed, and even Beauty offered her congratulations. "Though I might have won if I hadn't stumbled," she muttered.

So Rusty proudly pulled the king's carriage that evening, and he made such a good job of it that the king asked him if he would do it again the following year. Then the king asked Fred if his daughter could ride Beauty from time to time. He even gave Fred a bag of gold to pay for the horses' upkeep. So the three of them were happy as they never had been before as they returned home to the farm that night.

The Enchanted Harp

Long ago there lived a pedlar. Every day he took up the same place in the market square with his harp. Now this was no ordinary harp. It was an enchanted harp. The pedlar would call out to passersby and, for a penny, the harp would play all on its own any tune they wished. It could play any sort of tune from the slowest, most tearful ballad to the liveliest, happiest jig. It could play music for any occasion. Sometimes a wedding party would come by just to have the harp play a tune for the bride and groom.

Now one day a young man passed through the town. He heard the sound of the harp's sweet music coming from the market square and made his way over to where the pedlar stood. He couldn't believe his eyes or his ears! The harp was playing a lullaby for a lady with a baby that was crying. The music was so enchanting that the baby soon stopped wailing and was fast asleep. Then he saw an old man give the pedlar a penny and whisper in his ear. The harp changed its tune and now it played an ancient melody that the old man had not heard for many a year, and his eyes filled with tears of gratitude.

The young man watched all this and thought to himself, "If only that harp were mine. I could make a lot more money with it than that silly old pedlar!" He waited a while for the crowd to disperse, and then when he thought no-one was looking he went up to the pedlar and said, "People say that on this day a great spotted pig will fall out of the sky and land on the market square.

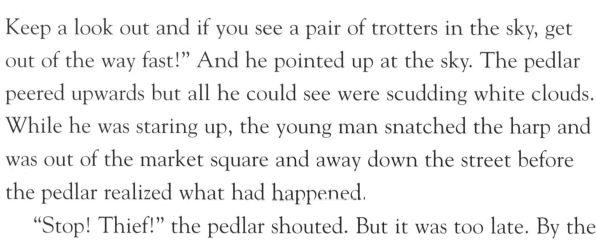

Keep a look out and if you see a pair of trotters in the sky, get out of the way fast!" And he pointed up at the sky. The pedlar peered upwards but all he could see were scudding white clouds. While he was staring up, the young man snatched the harp and was out of the market square and away down the street before the pedlar realized what had happened.

"Stop! Thief!" the pedlar shouted. But it was too late. By the time folk gave chase the young man had gone. He didn't stop running until he reached a town many miles away, where no-one had seen the enchanted harp before.

The young man set up the harp and called out to passersby, "Two pennies and my harp will play any tune you wish!" A man and woman came up and asked for a waltz and, sure enough, the harp began to play. The couple spun round the square merrily and were happy enough to give the young man two pennies.

More and more people came by and asked for tunes. The young man rubbed his hands with pleasure. "I shall surely make my fortune now," he said to himself.

Weeks passed and the young man did, indeed, make a lot of money. He didn't care at all how much he charged. If someone who looked wealthy came along he might charge them six pennies or even eight. By now he had completely forgotten that he had stolen the harp and that it didn't belong to him at all. He bought himself fine clothes and ate expensive food and generally considered himself rather clever.

Then one day an old man in a broad-brimmed hat came past and asked for a tune. He grumbled a bit when the young man asked for two pennies but held out the coins, making sure the young man could not see his face – for he was the pedlar!

"I'd like the harp to play a tune to drive you mad," said the old man. The young man thought this was a strange request but he had taken the coins and the harp had already started to play.

45

It played a short and very silly tune. Then it played it again. And again. And again. And again. It simply wouldn't stop. By now the old man had slipped away, so when people weren't watching the young man tried to kick the harp, but it side-stepped him and carried on playing. On and on it went, playing that infuriating tune. The young man put his hands over his ears to block out the noise, but the harp just played louder.

Passersby moved away. "What a terrible tune," they said. The young man tried to move away, too, but the harp just followed him down the road, still playing.

Everywhere he went, night and day, the harp followed the young man until he was at his wits' end. He had used up all his money and he was in despair. Finally, he thought there was only one thing to do. He must go back to the pedlar and beg him to stop the harp. It took him a while to make his way back to the town where the pedlar lived, but sure enough there he was, standing in the market square trying to sell a few old pots and pans to passersby. He looked very unhappy, and the young man felt truly sorry for what he had done.

He approached the pedlar with the harp still playing away behind him. He was about to explain when, to his surprise, the pedlar stopped him and said, "I know all about your plight. I will stop the harp playing its maddening tune on one condition."

"I'll do anything," said the young man.

"You must ask people what tune they would liked played and then you must give them a penny each time."

The young man gratefully agreed and the pedlar told the harp to stop playing. The young man had to work very hard to earn enough money to give people their pennies, but he was willing to do so in return for the pedlar making the harp stop playing that maddening tune!

 # The Golden Bird

There was once a king who kept a golden bird in a gilded cage. The bird wanted for nothing. Every day the king's servant brought him food and water and groomed his fine yellow feathers. And each day the bird sang his beautiful song for the king. "How lucky I am," cried the king, "to have such a beautiful bird that sings such a fine song." However, as time passed the king began to feel sorry for the bird. "It really isn't fair," he thought, "to keep such a handsome creature in a cage. I must give the bird its freedom." He called his servant and ordered him to take the cage into the jungle and release the bird.

48

The servant obeyed, and took the cage deep into the jungle where he came to a small clearing. He set the cage down, opened the door and out hopped the golden bird. "I hope you can look after yourself," the servant said as he walked away.

The golden bird looked about him. "This is strange!" he thought to himself. "Still, I suppose someone will come along to feed me soon." He settled down and waited.

After a while he heard a crashing sound in the trees, and then he saw a monkey swinging from branch to branch on his long arms.

"Hello there!" called the monkey, hanging by his tail and casting the bird an upside down grin. "Who are you?"

"I am the golden bird," replied the golden bird haughtily.

"I can see you're new around here," said the monkey. "I'll show you the best places to feed in the tree tops."

"No thanks," replied the golden bird ungratefully. "What could an ape like you possibly teach me? You've got such a funny face. I expect you're envious of my beautiful beak," he added.

"Have it your own way," called the monkey as he swung off into the trees.

Some time later the golden bird heard a hissing noise in the undergrowth and a snake came slithering by. "Well, hello," hissed the snake. "Who are you?"

"I am the golden bird," replied the golden bird proudly.

"Let me show you the jungle paths," said the snake.

"No thanks," replied the bird rudely. "What could a snake possibly teach me? With your horrid hissing voice, you must be jealous of my beautiful song," he said, forgetting that he had not opened his beak to sing yet.

"Very well," hissed the snake as he slithered away into the undergrowth.

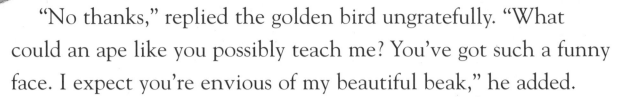

By now the golden bird was beginning to wonder when his food would arrive. He began to imagine the tasty morsel that he hoped he would soon be eating. Just then he was aware of a movement on the tree trunk behind him. Looking up he caught a glimpse of a chameleon, lying camouflaged against the trunk.

"Good day," said the chameleon. "I've been here all the time, so I know who you are. You're the golden bird. I've heard you say it twice. It's a good idea to know where to hide in case of danger. Let me show you."

"No thanks," replied the golden bird. "What could an ugly brute like you possibly teach me? You must wish you had lovely feathers like me," he said, fluffing up his beautiful, golden plumage.

"Don't say I didn't warn you," muttered the chameleon as he darted away.

The golden bird had just settled down again when a great gray shadow passed over the jungle. He looked up to see an eagle swooping low over the trees. The monkey swung up to hide in the densest foliage near the top of the trees. The snake slid into the deepest part of the undergrowth. The chameleon stayed quite still but his skin color became a perfect match for the tree he was on and he became totally invisible.

"Aha!" thought the golden bird. "All I have to do is fly away and that stupid eagle will never catch up with me." He flapped his wings and flapped and flapped, but he did not know that his wings had grown weak through living a life of luxury in the palace. Now the bird regretted his golden plumage and wished that he had dull brown feathers that would not show up in the forest clearing. For his fine yellow feathers made him easy to see. He was sure the eagle would come and gobble him up. "Help!" he trilled. "Please help me someone." Now he could see the eagle swooping down towards him with eyes blazing like fire and talons drawn.

At that moment the golden bird felt something close around his legs and pull him into the undergrowth. It was the snake. Then he was lifted up into the trees by a long, hairy arm and saw he was being carried by the monkey. "Keep still," whispered the chameleon pushing him into the center of a large yellow flower. "The eagle won't see you there." And sure enough, the golden bird found that he was precisely the color of the flower and the eagle flew straight past him.

"However can I repay you all?" exclaimed the bird. "You saved my life!"

"You can sing for us," replied the animals. And from then on, the monkey, the snake and the chameleon looked after the golden bird, and he sang his beautiful song for them every day.

The Boy Who Wished Too Much

There once was a young boy named Billy. He was a lucky lad, for he had parents who loved him, plenty of friends and a room full of toys. Behind his house was a trash heap. Billy had been forbidden to go there by his mother, but he used to stare at it out of the window. It looked such an exciting place to explore.

One day, Billy was staring at the trash heap, when he saw something gold-colored gleaming in the sunlight. There, on the top of the heap, sat a brass lamp. Now Billy knew the tale of Aladdin, and he wondered if this lamp could possibly be magic, too. When his mother wasn't looking he slipped out of the back door, scrambled up the heap and snatched the lamp from the top.

Billy ran to the backyard shed. It was quite dark inside, but Billy could see the brass of the lamp glowing softly in his hands. When his eyes had grown accustomed to the dark, he saw that the lamp was quite dirty. As he started to rub at the brass, there was a puff of smoke and the shed was filled with light. Billy closed his eyes tightly and when he opened them again, he found to his astonishment that there was a man standing there, dressed in a costume richly embroidered with gold and jewels. "I am the genie of the lamp," he said. "Are you by any chance Aladdin?"

"N… n… no, I'm Billy," stammered Billy, staring in disbelief.

"How very confusing," said the genie frowning. "I was told that the boy with the lamp was named Aladdin. Oh well, never mind! Now I'm here, I may as well grant you your wishes. You can have three, by the way."

At first Billy was so astonished he couldn't speak. Then he began to think hard. What would be the very best thing to wish for? He had an idea. "My first wish," he said, "is that I can have as many wishes as I want."

55

The genie looked rather taken aback, but then he smiled and said, "A wish is a wish. So be it!"

Billy could hardly believe his ears. Was he really going to get all his wishes granted? He decided to start with a really big wish, just in case the genie changed his mind later. "I wish I could have a purse that never runs out of money," he said.

Hey presto! There in his hand was a purse with five coins in it. Without remembering to thank the genie, Billy ran out of the shed and down the road to the candy store.

He bought a large bag of candy and took one of the coins out of his purse to pay for it. Then he peeped cautiously inside the purse, and sure enough there were still five coins. The magic had worked!

Billy ran back to the shed to get his next wish, but the genie had vanished. "That's not fair!" cried Billy, stamping his foot. Then he remembered the lamp. He seized it and rubbed at it furiously. Sure enough, the genie reappeared.

"Don't forget to share the candy with your friends," he said.

"What is your wish, Billy?"

This time Billy, who was very fond of sweet things, said, "I wish I had a house made of chocolate!"

No sooner had he uttered the words than he found that he was standing outside a house made entirely of rich, creamy chocolate. Billy broke off the door knocker and nibbled at it. Yes, it really was made of the most delicious chocolate that he had ever tasted! Billy gorged himself until he began to feel quite sick. He lay down on the grass and closed his eyes. When he opened them again, the chocolate house had vanished and he was outside the shed once more. "It's not fair to take my chocolate house away. I want it back!" he complained, stamping his foot once again.

Billy went back into the shed. "This time I'll ask for something that lasts longer," he thought. He rubbed the lamp and there stood the genie again.

"You've got chocolate all around your mouth," said the genie disapprovingly. "What is your wish?"

"I wish I had a magic carpet to take me to faraway lands," said Billy. No sooner were the words out of his mouth than he could feel himself being lifted up and out of the shed on a lovely soft carpet. The carpet took Billy up, up and away over hills, mountains and seas to the end of the Earth. He saw camels in the desert, polar bears at the North Pole and whales far out at sea. At last, Billy began to feel homesick and he asked the magic carpet to take him home. Soon he was back in his own backyard again.

Billy was beginning to feel very powerful and important. He began to wish for more and more things. He wished that he did not have to go to school – and so he didn't! He wished that he had a servant to clear up after him and a cook to make him special meals of sweet things – and a cook and a servant appeared.

58

Billy began to get very fat and lazy. His parents despaired at how spoiled he had become. His friends no longer came to play because he had grown so boastful.

One morning, Billy woke up, looked in the mirror and burst into tears. "I'm so lonely and unhappy!" he wailed. He realized that there was only one thing to do. He ran down to the backyard shed, picked up the lamp and rubbed it.

"You don't look very happy," said the genie, giving him a concerned glance. "What is your wish?"

"I wish everything was back to normal," Billy blurted out, "and I wish I could have no more wishes!"

"A wise choice!" said the genie. "So be it. Goodbye, Billy!" And with that the genie vanished. Billy stepped out of the shed, and from then on everything was normal again. His parents cared for him, he went to school and his friends came to play once more. But Billy had learned his lesson. He never boasted again and he always shared his candy and toys.

The Bee Who Wanted More Stripes

Bertie the bee was a rather vain young bee. Every morning, as soon as he woke up, he would find a large dewdrop in which to admire his reflection. The thing that Bertie liked best about himself was his stripes. He thought stripes were the smartest, flashiest fashion accessory any animal could have. He just wished he had more stripes. But he only had a couple. "Still," he thought, "they are very fine stripes."

Then he had an idea. What if he could get some more stripes? He would be the stripiest bee around, and then everyone else would admire him, too. "I know what I'll do," he said. "I'll ask some other very striped animals how they got all their stripes, and maybe I can copy them."

He buzzed off through the wood, looking for striped animals to ask. He flew across the fields and then the sea and at last he reached a place where there seemed to be quite a few striped animals. The first animal he approached looked like a striped horse. "Hello, neddy!" said Bertie, landing on the beast's nose.

"I'm not a horse – I'm a zebra. And get off my nose!" said the zebra crossly.

"I do beg your pardon," said Bertie. "I just wanted to ask you how you got your stripes."

"Well," said the zebra, "I used to be all brown. Then one day I came across a piano in the middle of the plain. As I walked past the piano, its black and white keys started to play a tune all by themselves. Then I looked down and found I had turned black and white, too. And if you believe that you'll believe anything!" And with that the zebra laughed and trotted off.

Bertie continued on his way. Now he could see a large striped cat. "Hello, puss!" said Bertie, landing on the creature's back.

"I'm not a cat – I'm a tiger. And get off my back!" growled the tiger.

"I'm so sorry," said Bertie, "I just wanted to ask you how you got your stripes."

"Well," said the tiger, "I used to be all yellow. Then one day, when I was a cub, I was playing with a ball of black string and I got all tangled up in it. And that's how I got my stripes. And if you believe that you'll believe anything!" And the tiger started to laugh as he stalked off.

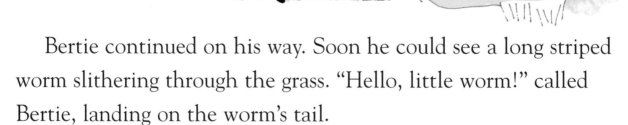

Bertie continued on his way. Soon he could see a long striped worm slithering through the grass. "Hello, little worm!" called Bertie, landing on the worm's tail.

"I'm not a worm – I'm a snake. And get off my tail!" hissed the snake.

"Oh dear. I didn't mean to upset you," said Bertie. "I just wanted to ask you how you got your stripes."

"Well," said the snake, "I used to be all brown. Then one day I was crossing a road just as the traffic lights were changing from red to green, and when I reached the other side I found that I was striped red and green from head to tail. And if you believe that you'll believe anything!" And the snake started to laugh as he slithered away.

Bertie continued on his way once more. Then he spotted a squirrel with a striped tail in a tree. "Hello, squirrel!" he said, landing on the animal's paw.

"I'm not a squirrel – I'm a ring-tailed lemur. And get off my paw!" said the ring-tailed lemur angrily.

"I do apologize," said Bertie. "I just wanted to ask you how you got your striped tail."

"Well," said the ring-tailed lemur, "my tail used to be all white. Then one day I was playing hoop-la with my friends. I said they could use my tail as a target, and so they threw all the rings on to my tail. But they got stuck. And that's how I got a striped tail. And if you believe that you'll believe anything!" And the ring-tailed lemur started to laugh as he scampered away.

"Well," thought Bertie, "I'd better give it a go!" First he looked for a piano on the plain, but to no avail. There just wasn't a piano to be found. Then he looked for a ball of string – but he couldn't find one of those, either. He did find a set of traffic lights and he buzzed backwards and forwards in front of them until he felt quite dizzy, but he still had the same number of stripes. Finally, he called out, "Anyone fancy a game of hoop-la?" But there was no reply. It was night time and all the animals were asleep.

"I'll just have to make my way home," thought Bertie sadly. He flew all through the night and arrived home exhausted in the morning.

Just then he met Clarice, the wise old bee. "Clarice," said Bertie, "I really would like some more stripes, but although I've asked lots of striped animals how they got their stripes, all they gave me were silly answers."

Clarice looked at Bertie rather sternly and said, "You only get the stripes you were born with, Bertie. And besides, do you know what you would be if you had more stripes? You would be a wasp!"

Bertie looked horrified. The last thing he wanted to be was a wasp. Wasps were always going around frightening and stinging everyone, and no-one liked them at all.

Bertie thought for a few moments and then said, "Perhaps having just a few stripes but being liked by others is better after all."

Bobby's Best Birthday Present

It was the morning of Bobby's birthday and he was very excited. When he came down to breakfast, there on the table was a big pile of presents. Bobby opened them one by one. There was a beautiful book with pictures of wild animals, a toy racing car and a baseball cap. Bobby was very pleased with his presents, but where was the present from his parents? "Close your eyes and hold out your hands!" said his mother. When he opened his eyes there was a large rectangular parcel in his hands. Bobby tore off the wrapping and inside was a box. And inside the box was a wonderful, shiny, electric train set.

For a moment, Bobby looked at the train set lying in the box. It was so lovely he could hardly bear to touch it. There was an engine and six cars all lying neatly on their sides. Bobby carefully lifted the engine out of the box. Then he set up the track and soon he had the train whizzing round his bedroom floor. Freddie the cat came in and watched the train going round. Round and round she watched it go, then one time when the train came past her she swiped at it with her paw and derailed it. The engine and the six cars came tumbling off the track and landed in a heap on the floor. "Look what you've done!" wailed Bobby as he picked up the train and reassembled it. The cars were undamaged, but the engine had hit the side of his bed and was badly dented.

Bobby was very upset. "My brand new train is ruined!" he cried.

"Don't worry, Bobby," said his mother, "we can't take it back to the store now, but we can take it to the toymender in the morning. I'm sure he'll make a good job of mending the engine and it'll look as good as new again." Bobby played with his racing car, he wore his new baseball cap and he read his new book, but really all he wanted to do was to play with his train set. He went to bed that night with the engine on the floor near his bed.

In the morning when Bobby woke up, the first thing he did was to look at the poor broken engine of his train set. He picked it up, expecting to see the buckled metal, but the engine was perfect. He couldn't believe his eyes! He ran to his parents. "Look, look!" he cried. They were as amazed as he was. The engine worked perfectly and Bobby played happily with his train set all day – but he made sure Freddie kept out of his room!

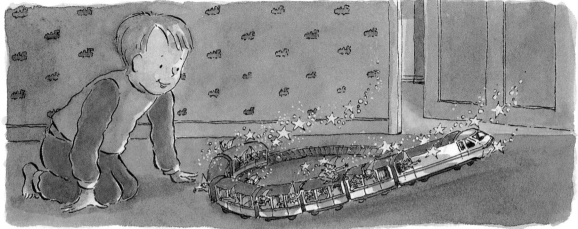

That night Bobby couldn't sleep. He lay in bed tossing and turning. Then he heard a noise. It was the sound of his train set rushing round the track. He peered into the darkness and yes, he could definitely make out the shape of the train as it sped by. How had the train started? It couldn't start all by itself! Had Freddie crept into his room and flicked the switch? As his eyes gradually became accustomed to the dark Bobby could make out several shapes sitting in the cars. Who were the mysterious passengers? He slid out of bed and on to the floor beside the train set. Now he could see that the passengers were little folk wearing strange pointed hats and leafy costumes. "Elves!" thought Bobby.

At that moment one of the elves spotted Bobby. "Hello there!" he called as the train rushed past again. "We saw that your train set was broken. We so much wanted a ride that we fixed it. I hope you don't mind!" Bobby was too astounded to say anything at all. "Come with us for a ride," called the elf as his car approached again.

As the train passed him the elf leaned out of the car and grabbed Bobby by the hand. Bobby felt himself shrinking as he flew through the air, and the next instant he was sitting beside the elf in the car of his very own train set! "Here we go – hold tight!" called the elf as the train left the track and went out through the window into the night sky.

"Now, where would you like to go? What would you like to see?" asked the elf.

"Toyland!" replied Bobby without hesitation. Sure enough, the train headed towards a track which curved up a mountain made of pink and white sugar. Beside the track were toys going about their daily business. Bobby saw a ragdoll getting into a shiny tin automobile. Then a wooden sailor puppet wound it up with a large key and off went the doll. He saw three teddy bears setting off for school with their satchels on their backs. Then he saw a brightly colored clown playing a drum.

The train stopped and Bobby and the elves got out. "Now for some fun!" said one of the elves. They had come to a halt by a toy fairground. Bobby found that this was like no other fairground he had ever been to before. For in Toyland, all the rides are real. The horses on the carousel were real horses. The dodgem cars were real cars. And when he got in the rocket for the rocket ride, it took him all the way to the moon and back!

"Time to go, Bobby," said one of the elves at last. "It'll be morning soon." Bobby climbed wearily back into the train and soon he was fast asleep. When he woke up it was morning, and he was back in his bed. The train set lay quite still on its tracks. But in one of the cars was a scrap of paper and on the paper, in tiny spidery writing, were the words: *We hope you enjoyed your trip to Toyland – the elves.*

Jimbo Comes Home

Jimbo the circus elephant was snoring away in his cage one night when he heard a strange noise. At first he thought it was part of his dream. In his dream he was walking across a hot, dusty plain while in the distance there was the sound of thunder.

All at once Jimbo was wide awake. He realized that he was in his cage after all and that what he thought was the sound of thunder was the noise of his cage on the move. Now this worried him, because the circus never moved at night. He rose to his feet and looked around. He could see men pulling on the tow bar at the front of the cage. These were strangers – it certainly wasn't Carlos his trainer! Jimbo started to bellow, "Help! Stop thief!" But it was too late. His cage was already rumbling out of the circus ground and down the road.

Eventually, the cage passed through a gate marked 'Zipper's Circus' and Jimbo knew what had happened. He had been stolen by the Zipper family, his own circus family's greatest rivals! Jimbo was furious. How had the thieves got away with it? Surely someone at Ronaldo's Circus must have heard them stealing him? But Jimbo waited in vain to be rescued.

The next morning, the thieves opened up Jimbo's cage and tried to coax him out, but he stayed put. In the end, after much struggling, they managed to pull him out. Once he was out of his cage, he took the biggest drink of water he could from a bucket and soaked his new keeper! He refused to cooperate, kicked over his food, and when he appeared in the circus that night he made sure he got all the tricks wrong.

"Don't worry," said Mr Zipper to Jimbo's new trainer, "he'll just take a little while to settle down. Soon he'll forget that he was once part of Ronaldo's Circus." But Jimbo didn't forget for, as you know, an elephant never forgets.

The other animals in Zipper's Circus had all been stolen from other circuses, too. "You'll just have to get used to it here," said one of the chimps to Jimbo. "It's not so bad really." But Jimbo decided he was going to try and escape.

One night, a mouse passed by his cage. "Hello," called Jimbo mournfully, for by now he was feeling very lonely, and no-one had cleaned his cage out for days.

"Hello!" said the mouse. "You don't look very happy. What's the matter?" Jimbo explained how he had been stolen and wanted to escape back to his own circus. The mouse listened and then said, "I'll try to help." So saying, he scampered off and soon he was back with a bunch of keys. Jimbo was astonished. "Easy!" said the mouse. "The keeper was asleep, so I helped myself."

Jimbo took the keys in his trunk and unlocked the door to the cage. He was free! "Thank you!" he called to the mouse, who was already scurrying away.

Jimbo's first thought was to get back to his own circus as fast as possible. However, he wanted to teach those thieves a lesson. He could hear them snoring in their caravan. He tiptoed up, as quietly as an elephant can tiptoe, and slid into the horse's harness at the front. "Hey, what do you think you're doing?"

neighed one of the horses, but Jimbo was already hauling the robbers' caravan out of the gate and down the road.

So gently did he pull the caravan that the thieves never once woke up. Eventually they reached Ronaldo's Circus. Mr Ronaldo was dumbstruck to see Jimbo pulling a caravan just like a horse! Mr Ronaldo walked over to the caravan and was astonished to see the robbers still fast asleep. He raced to the telephone and called the police, and it wasn't until they heard the police siren that the robbers woke up. By then it was too late. As they emerged from the caravan scratching and shaking their heads they were arrested on the spot and taken off to jail. "There are a few questions we would like to ask Mr Zipper regarding the theft of some other circus animals, too," said one of the police officers.

Mr Ronaldo, and Jimbo's keeper Carlos, were both delighted to see Jimbo back home again. And Jimbo was just as delighted to be back home. Then Mr Ronaldo and Carlos started whispering to each other and began walking away looking secretive. "We'll be back soon, we promise," they said to Jimbo. When they returned, they were pushing Jimbo's old cage. It had been freshly painted, there was clean, sweet-smelling straw inside, but best of all there was no lock on the door! "Now you can come and go as you please," said Carlos.

And Jimbo trumpeted long and loud with his trunk held high, which Carlos knew was his way of saying, "THANK YOU!"

The Lonely Mermaid

There once lived a mermaid named Miriam who was very lonely. All day long she sat on a rock combing her long, yellow hair and singing to herself. Sometimes she would flick her beautiful turquoise fish tail in the water and watch the ripples spreading far out to sea. Miriam had not always been lonely. In fact, she used to have a pair of playmates called Octopus and Dolphin. Octopus had gone off to another part of the ocean to work for the Sea King. He was always much in demand because he could do eight jobs at once – one with each arm. Dolphin, meanwhile, had gone away to teach singing in a school of dolphins. Miriam once thought she heard his lovely song far away across the ocean and she hoped in vain that he might come back and play.

One day Miriam was sitting on her favorite rock as usual. "How lonely I am," she sighed to her reflection as she combed her hair and gazed at herself in the mirror.

To her astonishment, her reflection seemed to answer back. "Don't be lonely," said a voice. "Come and play with me."

Miriam couldn't understand it at all. She peered into the mirror and then she saw, beyond her own reflection, another mermaid! She was so startled that she dropped the mirror and her comb and spun around.

Miriam was puzzled by the sight in front of her. For there, sitting on the next rock was another mermaid – and yet she didn't look like a mermaid in many ways. She had short, dark, curly hair and wore a strange costume that definitely wasn't made of seaweed. When Miriam looked down to where the mermaid's fish tail should have been, she wanted to burst out laughing.

For instead of a beautiful tail, the other mermaid had two strange limbs like an extra long pair of arms stretching down.

The other 'mermaid', who was really a little girl called Georgie, was equally amazed by the sight of Miriam. She had seen pictures of mermaids in books before, but now she couldn't quite believe her eyes. For here, on the rock beside her, was a real live mermaid!

For a moment they were both too astonished to speak. Then they both said at once, "Who are you?"

"I'm Miriam," said Miriam.

"I'm Georgie," said Georgie.

"Let's go for a swim," said Miriam. Soon the two of them were in the water, chasing each other and giggling.

"Let's play tag along the beach," suggested Georgie, and started swimming towards the shore. She had quite forgotten that Miriam would not be able to run around on dry land. Miriam followed though she was rather afraid, as her mother had always told her not to go near the shore in case she got stranded. Georgie ran out of the water and up on to the beach.

"Wait for me!" called Miriam, struggling in the water as her tail thrashed about. Then, to her astonishment, something strange happened. She found she could leave the water with ease and, looking down, saw that her tail had disappeared and that in its place were two of those strange long arm things like Georgie's.

"What's happened?" she wailed.

Georgie looked round. "You've grown legs!" she shouted in amazement. "Now you can play tag!"

Miriam found that she rather liked having legs. She tried jumping in the air, and Georgie taught her to hop and skip. "You can come and stay at my house, but first I must find you some clothes," said Georgie, looking at Miriam who was wearing nothing but her long, yellow hair. "Wait for me here!"

Georgie ran off and soon she was back with a tee shirt and shorts. Miriam put them on. They ran back to Georgie's house together. "This is my friend Miriam," said Georgie to her mother. "Can she stay for tea?"

"Why, of course," said Georgie's mother.

"What's that strange thing?" whispered Miriam.

"It's a chair," said Georgie. She showed Miriam how to sit on the chair. All through teatime Miriam watched Georgie to see how she should eat from a plate and drink from a cup and saucer. She'd never tasted food like this before. How she wished she could have chocolate cake at home under the sea!

After tea Miriam said, "Now I'll show *you* how to do something." Taking Georgie by the hand she led her down to the beach again. There they picked up shells, and then Miriam showed Georgie how to make a lovely necklace from shells threaded with seaweed. While they made their necklaces, Miriam taught Georgie how to sing songs of the sea.

Soon it was bedtime. "You can sleep in the spare bed in my room," said Georgie. Miriam slipped in between the sheets. How strange it felt! She was used to feeling water all around her and here she was lying in a bed. She tossed and turned, feeling hotter and hotter, and couldn't sleep at all. In the middle of the night she got up and threw open the window to get some fresh air.

She could smell the salty sea air and she began to feel rather homesick. Then she heard a familiar sound from far away. It was Dolphin calling to her! The noise was getting closer and closer until at last Miriam knew what she must do. She slipped out of the house and ran down to the beach in the moonlight. As soon as her toes touched the water, her legs turned back into a fish tail and she swam out to sea to join Dolphin.

The next morning, when Georgie woke up, she was very upset to find that her friend had gone. When she told her mother who Miriam really was, her mother said, "The sea is a mermaid's true home and that's where she belongs. But I'm sure you two will always be friends."

And indeed, from time to time, Georgie was sure that she could see Miriam waving to her from the sea.

Mr Squirrel Won't Sleep

It was fall. The leaves were dropping from the trees in the forest and there was a cold nip in the air. All the animals began to get ready for winter.

One night Mr Fox came back from hunting and said to his wife, "There's not much food about now it's getting colder. We'd better start storing what we can to help tide us over the winter."

"You're right, Mr Fox," replied his wife, as she gathered her cubs into their lair.

"I'd love to go fishing," said Mr Bear, "but I'll have to wait until spring now." He went into his den, shut the door tight and sealed it.

"Well, I'm off for a holiday in the sun," announced Mrs Cuckoo, preening her feathers. "See you all next year!" she called as she took to the wing and flew south.

Mrs Mouse ran by with a mouthful of straw. "Must dash," she squeaked, "or my winter bed will never be finished in time." But soon she, too, was curled up with her tail wrapped around her for warmth.

Now only Mr Squirrel wasn't ready for winter. He danced about in his tree, leaping from branch to branch and chasing his tail. "Ha, ha!" he boasted. "I don't have to get ready for winter. I have a fine store of nuts hidden away, a beautiful bushy tail to keep me warm and besides, I don't feel in the least bit sleepy." And he carried on playing in his tree.

"Are you still awake?" snapped Mr Fox.

"Go to sleep!" growled Mr Bear.

"Please be quiet," squeaked Mrs Mouse, drawing her tail more tightly about her ears.

But Mr Squirrel wouldn't go to sleep. Not a bit of it. He danced up and down all the more and shouted, "I'm having SUCH FUN!" at the top of his voice.

Winter came. The wind whistled in the trees' bare branches, the sky turned gray and it became bitterly cold. Then it started to snow. At first Mr Squirrel had a grand time making snowballs – but there was no-one around to throw them at and he began to feel rather lonely. Soon he felt cold and hungry, too.

"No problem!" he said to himself. "I'll have some nice nuts to eat. Now, where did I bury them?" He scampered down his tree to find that the ground was deep with snow. He ran this way and that trying to find his hiding places, but all the forest looked the same in the snow and soon he was hopelessly lost.

"Whatever shall I do?" he whimpered, for now he was shivering with cold and hunger and his beautiful, bushy tail was all wet and bedraggled.

All of a sudden he thought he heard a small voice. But where was it coming from? He looked all around but there was no sign of anyone. Then he realized that the voice was coming from under the snow. "Hurry up!" said the voice. "You can join me down here, but you'll have to dig a path to my door."

Mr Squirrel started digging frantically with his front paws and sure enough there was a path leading to a door under a tree stump. The door was slightly open – open enough for Mr Squirrel to squeeze his thin, tired body through.

Inside was a warm, cosy room with a roaring fire, and sitting by the fire was a tiny elf. "I heard you running around up there and thought you might be in need of a bit of shelter," said the elf. "Come and warm yourself by the fire." Mr Squirrel was only too pleased to accept and soon he was feeling warm and dry.

"This isn't my house, you know," said the elf. "I think it might be part of an old badgers' sett. I got lost in the forest and so when I found this place, I decided to stay here until spring. Though how I'll ever find my way home, I don't know." A fat tear rolled down the elf's cheek.

"I have been a very foolish squirrel," said Mr Squirrel. "If you hadn't taken me in I surely would have died. I am indebted to you and if you will let me stay here until spring, I will help you find your way home."

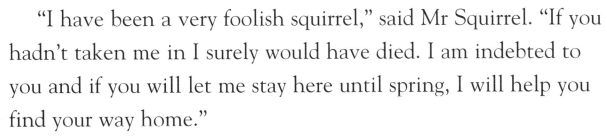

"Of course you can stay," replied the elf. "I'd be glad of the company." So Mr Squirrel settled down with his tail for a blanket and soon he was fast asleep.

Days and nights passed, until one day the elf popped his head out of the door and exclaimed, "The snow has melted, spring is coming. Wake up, Mr Squirrel." Mr Squirrel rubbed his eyes and looked out. It was true. There were patches of blue in the sky and he could hear a bird singing.

"Climb upon my back," Mr Squirrel said to the elf. "I'm going to show you the world." They set off through the forest until they came to the highest tree of all.

"Hold tight!" called Mr Squirrel as he climbed up through the branches until finally they reached the very top of the tree.

"You can look now," said Mr Squirrel, seeing that the elf had put his tiny hands over his eyes. The elf uncovered his eyes and stared and stared. He had never seen anything like it in his whole life. Stretching in all directions, as far as the eye could see, were mountains, lakes, rivers, forests and fields.

"What's that silvery-blue thing in the distance?" asked the elf.

"Why, that's the sea!" replied Mr Squirrel.

Suddenly the elf started to jump for joy.

"What is it?" said Mr Squirrel.

"I… I… can see my home," cried the elf, pointing down into the valley below the forest. "And there's my wife sitting in a chair in the sunshine. I must go home, Mr Squirrel. Thank you for showing me the world, for I should never have seen my home again without you." And with that he climbed down the tree and skipped all the way home.

Mr Squirrel made his way back to his own tree.

"Where have you been?" said Mr Fox.

"We've been looking for you," said Mr Bear.

"I'm glad you're home," said Mrs Mouse.

"So am I," said Mr Squirrel. "I've been very foolish, but I've learned my lesson. Now let's have a party – I've got rather a lot of nuts that need eating up!"

So the animals celebrated spring with a fine feast.

And Mr Squirrel vowed not to be silly again next winter.

The Bear and the Ice Kingdom

Once upon a time a king ruled a far-off land. It was a sunny, pleasant kingdom with lush forests, green meadows and sparkling rivers. The king of this land had a daughter he loved very much, and who one day would rule the kingdom.

Beyond the king's land was another kingdom, but this one was very different. It was an icy-cold place with wind-swept, snowy plains and cold, frozen seas. The sun never warmed this kingdom, and it was always winter. Anyone or anything venturing into the kingdom was immediately turned to ice by the cold. This kingdom was ruled by a wicked ogre, whose wish was to own the warm lands of his neighbor.

One day the wicked ogre thought of a cunning plan to capture the kingdom he desired. He decided he would kidnap the king's daughter. Once she had entered the wicked ogre's ice kingdom she, too, would be turned to ice. In time, the king would die and, as there would be no-one to inherit his kingdom, the wicked ogre could seize it.

So one day, the wicked ogre left his own cold kingdom and traveled to the other kingdom disguised as a merchant. He carried a big bag containing some samples of cloth and some jewelry. The wicked ogre came to the castle gates and asked if he might show the princess his wares. She agreed, and showed him to a room where he laid out the cloth and jewelry on a table. But as soon as she started to look at the wares, the wicked ogre bundled her up in the bag and carried her off.

As soon as the princess felt the cold chill of the wicked ogre's kingdom, she was immediately frozen to ice.

The wicked ogre thought that all he now had to do was wait for the king to die of old age or a broken heart, and the kingdom would be his. But despite the cunning of the wicked ogre, his evil deed had been spotted by one of the king's courtiers. The king immediately sent his troops to the ice kingdom to rescue his daughter. But as soon as they reached the kingdom they, too, were frozen to ice.

The king was in despair. There seemed to be no way to get his beloved daughter back. Then one day he thought of an idea. He sent out a royal proclamation to every part of his land. It said that anyone who could rescue his daughter would be granted any gift within the king's power to bestow.

Many adventurers tried to rescue the king's daughter, in the hope that they might win her hand in marriage, or be granted riches and lands as a reward. But each who ventured into the evil ogre's ice kingdom met the same fate. All were turned to ice.

Then one day, the king's dancing bear read the royal proclamation and asked to speak with the king. "Your majesty," said the dancing bear, "I have a plan to rescue your daughter, the princess."

"And what is your plan?" asked the king.

"My plan is a secret, your majesty," said the dancing bear. "But if you will trust me, I promise she will be brought safely home."

The king agreed to let the dancing bear try and rescue his daughter. After all, every other attempt had ended in failure so what did he have to lose? The dancing bear was released from his chain and went off immediately to begin his task. He traveled day and night until finally he reached his destination – a cold, snowy place where his cousin lived. His cousin was not like the dancing bear, however. The dancing bear was small and brown, but his cousin was big and white. This bear loved the cold and snow, for he had a thick fur coat. He was a polar bear.

The dancing bear told his cousin what had befallen the king's daughter. The polar bear agreed to rescue her. The dancing bear couldn't wait to get going, for his cousin's snowy home was much too cold for him. Eventually they arrived back in the king's land, and the polar bear set off alone to try and rescue the princess.

Soon he reached the wicked ogre's ice kingdom. A freezing, icy wind blew all around the polar bear, but his thick, warm fur coat kept out the cold. Then a huge snow storm came up, but the polar bear just shook his fur and all the snow fell from him. On went the polar bear until he reached the wicked ogre's castle.

The ogre never expected that anyone would be able to enter his cold kingdom without being turned to ice, so he never even locked his doors. While the ogre was snoring in his bedroom, the polar bear searched stealthily around the castle until he found the frozen princess. He gently gathered her up, and they were just about to make their escape when the ogre awoke.

As the wicked ogre tried to snatch the princess away from the polar bear, the polar bear dealt the wicked ogre a mighty blow with his paw. The wicked ogre fell down dead. The polar bear then carried the princess away from the icy kingdom. As soon as she entered her father's warm kingdom again, she returned to life.

There was much rejoicing at the return of the king's daughter, of course, and the first thing the king did was to summon the dancing bear to him.

"You have kept your promise," the king said, "and now I will keep mine. What is your wish?"

"All I ask, your majesty, is that I am freed to roam the forests of your kingdom."

The king immediately granted his wish. And as a reward to the polar bear, he was given the ice kingdom as his own domain which, being so cold, suited him just fine!